The
Southernmost
Cat

By John Cech
Illustrated by Kathy Osborn

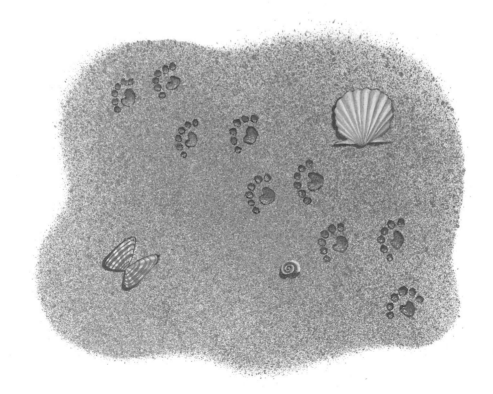

Simon & Schuster Books for Young Readers

SIMON & SCHUSTER BOOKS FOR YOUNG READERS
An imprint of Simon & Schuster Children's Publishing Division
1230 Avenue of the Americas, New York, NY 10020
Text copyright © 1996 by John Cech
Illustrations copyright © 1996 by Kathy Osborn
All rights reserved including the right of reproduction
in whole or in part in any form.
SIMON & SCHUSTER BOOKS FOR YOUNG READERS
is a trademark of Simon & Schuster.
Designed by Paul Zakris and Christy Hale
The text of this book is set in 15-point Goudy Sans Medium.
The illustrations are rendered in gouache.
Manufactured in the United States of America.
10 9 8 7 6 5 4 3 2 1
Library of Congress Cataloging-in-Publication Data
Cech, John.
The Southernmost Cat / by John Cech ; illustrated by Kathy
Osborn. — 1st ed., 1st American ed.
p.   cm.
Summary: While being dragged around the Atlantic Ocean by a
huge fish, an adventuresome cat, whose life bears an amazing
resemblance to that of Ernest Hemingway, recalls the events of
his previous eight existences.
ISBN 0-689-80510-1
[1.Cats—Fiction. 2. Fishes—Fiction. 3. Adventure and
adventurers—Fiction. 4. Hemingway, Ernest, 1899–
1961—Fiction.]
I. Osborn, Kathy, ill. II. Title.
PZ7.C29975So   1996   [E]—dc20   93-40671

"LIFE IS GOOD," thought the Southernmost Cat.

He sat in his boat off Key West, off the southernmost point of the southernmost island of the southernmost part of the country. He had a good, sturdy line swaying in the calm water, and the light was playing on the smooth surface.

"Life is good because the sky is turning pink and blue and yellow, and a tang of salt and seaweed is filling the air, and the warm breeze is rolling all the way from Mexico across the gulf.

"It is good because I still have most of my tail and all of my whiskers and six toes on every paw. And later I will see my friends, and we will drink something cool in a café on Duvall Street and watch the tourists go by.

"But I have not caught a fish in weeks. I'm all out of peanut butter and pretzels, I've finished the prunes and the pickles. And if I don't catch a fish, I won't have anything to eat, and that is not good."

The Southernmost Cat waited all morning for a nibble.
But his line just swayed slowly in the smooth water, and
he drifted further and further out to sea.

His friends called to him from shore, "Ernesto! Come to
lunch with us! Our treat!"

But he waved them away. "It is important," he thought,
"that a cat should catch his own lunch."

The Southernmost Cat thought about the lives he had already used up out of the nine lives every cat gets to live.

He thought about the time he ran with the bulls in Pamplona, wearing his red bandanna, with the bulls snorting and clattering over the cobblestones right behind him. That was one life.

He thought about the time he swam around the channel, the sharks nipping at his heels all the way. That was life number two.

Then there was the time he ate all 471 of Alice B.'s
infamous brownies on a dare and wandered in a daze
through Paris for a week. That was three.

"If I have to sit much longer, I'll bake up my last life here
in the sun," he thought to himself.

But just as he was nodding off in the midday heat, the line snapped straight. And the little skiff leaped forward, throwing the Southernmost Cat to the bottom of the boat. He held on to the line for dear life, his rear paws braced against the boat's bow.

"Carumba! It's a big one!" he sputtered as the fish pulled him out to sea.

It pulled, it pulled. It pulled all through the afternoon and into the evening. But the Southernmost Cat could not see the fish that was pulling him. It was swimming too deep under the water.

"I wonder what kind of fish it is to pull my boat along like this," thought the Southernmost Cat. Then he called out to the fish, "Oh, fish, listen to me. You must be a mighty fish, but you do not know who you are pulling, do you? Do you know that you are pulling a cat who was carried by a hurricane for three hundred miles and still landed on his feet? Do you know that I have been to the North Pole and back in a blizzard with only a box of raisins to eat? Do you know that I have ridden across Caracas in rush hour on a bicycle with two flat tires? And do you know that I am the finest fisherman of the southernmost point?"

The Southernmost Cat stayed awake all night while the fish kept pulling the boat north. Early in the morning, the fish pulled the boat through the Bermuda Triangle, where the Southernmost Cat saw some very strange things—how long he was there, he could not say.

The fish pulled the cat and his boat past great cities, their lights sparkling on the distant horizon, and north through a sea of icebergs, then south around green islands, past the tall chalk cliffs where the sun also rises, and further south.

"Oh, fish, you are a very powerful fish," the Southernmost Cat cried out. Now he could see the enormous shape of the fish faintly under the water. "You will not give up, and neither will I. We must truly be brothers, fish. But that does not mean that Ernesto will not catch you in the end!"

So the Southernmost Cat held on. He had not eaten for days, and the only water he had to drink came from raindrops that pattered on his tongue. His paws were raw and his shoulders ached, but he refused to let the fish take even an inch more of the line.

The fish swam strongly on, pulling the cat and his boat down to Africa. The Southernmost Cat thought about the last two lives he had used. He thought about the furious rhinoceros that chased him through Kenya.

And he thought about the top of Mount Kilimanjaro, how he climbed to its snowy top, where everything was frozen.

And as he was thinking, the fish suddenly took a sharp right turn and they headed west.

"Oh, fish," the Southernmost Cat called, "you are very clever. But now I will show you who is smarter!"

Mustering all his strength, the cat began to haul in the line. It was hard work, inch by painful inch, and he was at it for hours, even though his muscles burned. The more line he pulled in, the closer the fish swam to the surface. Then he could finally see the fish, all white and then more white, a mountain of white, leap from the water, huge and towering, water spouting.

"Oh, fish! You are bigger than big. All the more reason to catch you!" the Southernmost Cat yelled as he yanked as hard as he could on the line.

The fish leaped and spun and twirled in the air. Still the cat held on. He even held on when the fish circled the boat, making huge waves that lifted the craft and threw it down again, breaking it into splinters. The cat clung to a piece of the boat as the fish swam toward him, its huge mouth open.

Then the fish did an amazing thing. It spoke.

"You're a brave one," boomed the fish. "Small, but brave. And persistent. My right fin hurts from your hook, and I really should flatten you with my tail."

"As you wish," said the Southernmost Cat defiantly. "It has been a good run. I've had eight lives already, and I can't think of a better way to spend my last one."

"Eight lives? That's interesting," the fish burbled deeply.

"Yes, it's quite a story," said the Southernmost Cat.

"You know," the fish replied, "I haven't heard a good tale for a century. Tell me yours, and then later we'll see about turning you into flotsam and jetsam."

So the Southernmost Cat sat on the fish's flat, white
head and told it the stories of his lives. And as they were
finishing the last story about the snowcapped mountain,
they came into the harbor of the southernmost place. It
was sunset, and the whole town had turned out to watch
for the flash of green at the very end.

Ernesto's friends were there, too. They had come to
watch the sunset and to shed a tear or two for their lost
friend. There were Zelda and Scotty, Gertrude and Alice B.,
and Tennessee and Langston and Herman and Emily and
Nathaniel and Zora and Sherwood and Eudora and Norman.
They had many spent lives among them.

The fish told the Southernmost Cat, "You know, you tell a good story."

"Well, what does it matter? You're just going to turn me into smithereens anyway."

"Not if you'll promise to do something for me."

"What's that?"

"Stay away from fishing."

"But . . . "

"Try writing instead."

"About what?"

"Tell your stories. And send me a copy when you're done."

"How will I do that?"

"Just float it out on the tide, and I'll get it."

And with that, the fish sent the Southernmost Cat sailing to shore in a spout of water.

"Ernesto! You're back!" Scotty cried.

"We thought you'd finally checked out," said Herman.

"This calls for a celebration," Tennessee proclaimed. "Come to the café and tell us about your ordeal."

"No, not now. Tomorrow," said the Southernmost Cat as he said his good nights to his friends.

But the Southernmost Cat did not want to sleep.
Something else was stirring. Something would slip away
if he went to the café. He wanted to write it all down first
before he told anyone about his ninth life. So he went
home and stood at his typewriter and thought for a
moment, and then he wound a sheet of paper into it and
typed: "Life is good." And he didn't stop typing until he
was done.

A Note on the Story

If you take Route 1 as far as it will go, past the Everglades, with its egrets and cranes and snapping alligators, and over the Seven-Mile Bridge, you will arrive at a cone-shaped concrete marker on the island of Key West. A six-toed cat may be sleeping on the corner post of the nearby fence that surrounds the Southernmost House. At least one was when I was there. I petted the cat and looked at the sign on the marker that proclaimed "The Southernmost Point" (it really does), and called to my wife: "Then this must be the Southernmost Cat!" The cat barely stirred, unimpressed, but he let us take his picture. When last I heard, there were 49 six-toed cats on the island, all of them descendants of the cat that belonged to the famous American writer Ernest Hemingway, who lived in Key West and to whom this story is offered as a whiskery homage.

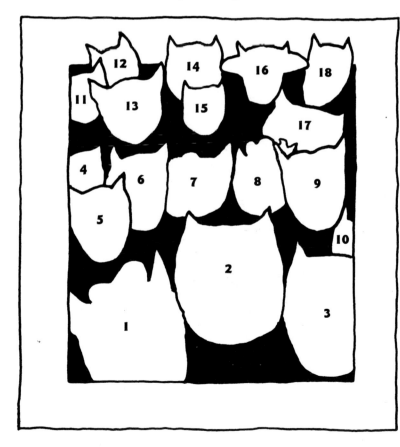

The names of the Southernmost Cat's companions were inspired by real writers of the nineteenth and twentieth centuries, many of whom were friendly with Ernest Hemingway himself. Here is a key to these imaginary and very literary cats who make a group appearance in the painting on page 35.

1. Walt Whitman
2. Mark Twain
3. Tennessee Williams
4. Kathy Osborn's cat, Buddy
5. Stephen Crane
6. Eudora Welty
7. Alice B. Toklas
8. Gertrude Stein
9. F. Scott Fitzgerald
10. Zelda Fitzgerald
11. Herman Melville
12. Langston Hughes
13. Ezra Pound
14. Louisa May Alcott
15. Emily Dickinson
16. Zora Neale Hurston
17. Sherwood Anderson
18. Nathaniel Hawthorne